TWIT TWOO

The owl who was nearly magic

By Steve Cole

Illustrated by Jane Porter

Orion
Children's Books

First published in Great Britain in 2015
by Orion Children's Books
An imprint of Hachette Children's Group
Part of Hodder & Stoughton
Carmelite House
50 Victoria Embankment
London EC4Y 0DZ
An Hachette UK Company

Text © Steve Cole 2015
Illustrations © Jane Porter 2015

A CIP catalogue record for this book
is available from the British Library.

ISBN 978 1 4440 1344 3

2 4 6 8 10 9 7 5 3 1

Printed and bound in China

www.orionchildrensbooks.co.uk

TWIT TWOO

The owl who was
nearly magic

There are lots of Early Reader
stories you might enjoy.

Look at the back of the book or,
for a complete list, visit
www.orionchildrensbooks.co.uk

For Freya Kittel – S.C.
For John Murran with love – J.P.

Contents

Chapter One

There was once a little owl
who wasn't very wise.
His name was Twit.

He had wide eyes. Scruffy
feathers. A kind heart.

And three brothers –

Boggle,

Bumf

and Baffle
    – who liked to
    play tricks on him.

One night, the moon was
shining very bright.
"The moon's in my eyes,"
Bumf complained. "Turn
it off, Twit."

"There's a long string hanging down from the moon," said Boggle, giggling. "Pull it and the light goes out."

"Then we'll all sleep better,"
said Twit. "What a good idea!"

But of course, no one can
turn off the moon.

Twit didn't know that. Off
he flapped, trying to reach
the moon.
He flew round and about.
Higher and higher. This way
and that.

Twit's little wings grew tired.
He perched in a tree to catch
his breath, and quickly fell
asleep.

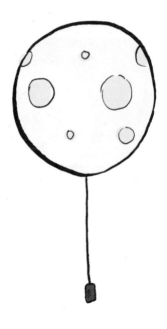

Chapter Two

At sunrise, Twit opened his
eyes.
"Where am I?" he said
sleepily.

Twit had flown right out of
the wood!
A line of wagons had stopped
along the road below him.
A sign on the front said
BONGO'S
TRAVELLING
CIRCUS.

The circus ringmaster looked very worried. "Two of the animals are missing!" he said. "We must find them."

Twit decided to fly back
home.
As he flitted from tree to
tree, the wood seemed very
empty.

Twit dropped in on his
friend, Norma the vole.
The door was open, but she
was not at home.
"That's funny," thought Twit.

Twit flew deeper and deeper
into the wood. He did not see
anyone at all.
The squirrel in his tree
had gone.

The stoat in his den – gone.

Even the bear in her cave –
gone.

The whole wood was empty.
"Has everyone gone on
holiday?" Twit wondered.

But when he reached home,
he **did** see someone.
Two very unexpected
someones.

A lion and a crocodile!

Chapter Three

"Hello!" Twit gasped.
"I'm Twit. Who are you?"

"My name is Chomp," said
the lion.
"And I am Snippy," said the
crocodile.

"What an unfriendly wood!"
said Chomp. "All the other
animals ran away when they
saw us."
"So that is why the wood is
empty," Twit thought.

"Please don't run away,"
said Chomp. "We love
eating birds."
"Oooohhhhhh!"
Twit twittered.
"Er, we love meeting
birds," said Snippy quickly.

Twit blinked. "Are you from
that circus?"
"Yes, we are." Snippy smiled.
"We are putting on a special
magic show here in the
wood."

"Look!" Chomp pulled
three owls from behind
his back and started
juggling with them.

"My brothers!" Twit gasped.
"They're fast asleep!"
"They fainted at the sight of
us," Snippy said.

"It's a shame," Chomp grinned.
"For our big trick, Snippy and
I are going to make some
delicious bird food appear!"

"Bird food?" Twit rubbed his tummy. "Ooooh, lovely. What a good idea!"
But of course, it wasn't.

Chapter Four

"Wait!" Snippy held up a claw.

"This trick would taste much nicer – erm, I mean, it would work much better – with some salt and pepper from the circus kitchen."

Twit frowned. "I never heard of magic needing salt and pepper."

"We can't show you the bird food trick without it," said Snippy. "Why don't you sneak back and get some?" "What a good idea!" Twit hooted.

But of course, it wasn't. It really, really wasn't.

So, poor Twit flew back to
the circus. There were lots of
men running about now.

The kitchen was empty.
Twit found some salt and
pepper and flew off again.

The ringmaster shouted at
him. Twit kept going.

But there was one thing he
didn't notice . . .

Chapter Five

When Twit came back,
Snippy snatched the salt and
pepper and sprinkled them
over Twit's brothers.

"There's hardly any salt left!"
Snippy said.
"Plenty of pepper though,"
said Chomp, pouring it over
the three sleeping owls.

"Now we just need some berries!"

"Yes." Snippy gave Twit a sharp-toothed smile. "The trick won't taste delicious – erm, I mean, it won't work as well without berries."

Twit thought hard. "I saw some berries on a bush not far from here."

"Go and fetch them," said
Chomp.
"What a good idea!" cried Twit.

But of course, it wasn't.
It really, really wasn't.

Twit gathered the best
berries he could find and
back he went.
"Will the magic work now?"
Twit asked excitedly.

"Oh, yes." Snippy squished berries all over Boggle, Bumf and Baffle. "Now we're ready to start our big magic trick."

"Yes!" Chomp grinned. "Time to make four owls disappear – and *re*appear in our **tummies!**"

Chapter Six

With a **roar**, Snippy and Chomp rushed at Twit . . .

But just then the men from the circus burst out of the bushes, holding special nets!

Chomp and Snippy
snapped

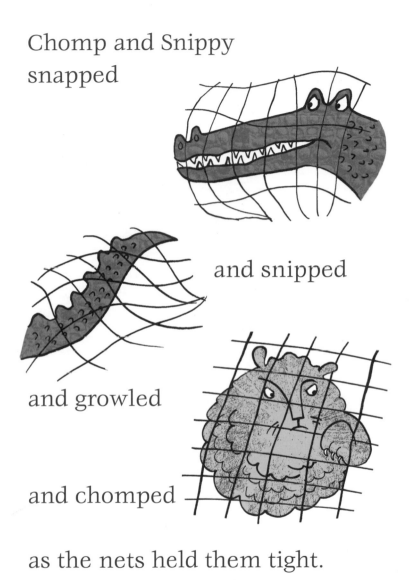

and snipped

and growled

and chomped

as the nets held them tight.

Chomp roared crossly.
"Not fair!"

Snippy snapped. "How did
you find us?"

"We followed a trail of salt!"
The ringmaster smiled at
Twit. "This clever owl carried
the salt upside down. He led
us right to you."

"But he's a twit!" said Bumf,
Baffle and Boggle.

"You three look like the twits to me," said the ringmaster. "Look at you, covered in salt and pepper and berries!"

The other animals had slowly
come back into the wood.
"Hooray for Twit!" cried
Norma the vole. "He made
our home safe again!"

"Hip, hip, hooray!"
called all the animals, as
Snippy and Chomp were led
back to the circus.

"How did I manage to save
the day?" Twit marvelled.

"By being yourself, Twit."
Norma gave him a hug.
"I think you're the most
magical owl in the world!"

And of course, Twit was.
He really, really was.

What are you going to read next?

Have more adventures with
Horrid Henry,

or save the day with Anthony Ant!

Become a
superhero with Monstar,

float off to
sea with
Algy,

or have your very own Pirates' Picnic.

Grow carrots with

Lottie and Dottie,

make magic with The Witch Dog,

and cast a spell with

The Three Little Magicians.

Enjoy all the Early Readers.